5

6

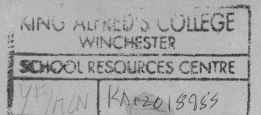
For Denise and Klaus

First published in hardback in Great Britain
by Andersen Press Ltd in 1994
First published in paperback by Picture Lions in 1996
This edition published by Collins Picture Books in 2002

1 3 5 7 9 10 8 6 4 2
ISBN: 0-00-714013-4

Picture Lions and Collins Picture Books are imprints of the
Children's Division, part of HarperCollins Publishers Ltd.
Text and illustrations copyright © Colin McNaughton 1994
The author/illustrator asserts the moral right to be identified
as the author/illustrator of the work.
A CIP catalogue record for this title is available
from the British Library.

The HarperCollins website address is: www.fireandwater.com

Printed in Hong Kong

Colin McNaughton
Suddenly!

Collins

An imprint of HarperCollinsPublishers

Preston was walking home
from school one day when

suddenly!

Preston remembered
his mum had asked
him to go to the shops.

Preston was doing
the shopping when

suddenly!

He dashed out of the
shop! (He remembered
he had left the shopping
money in his school desk.)

Ah, there it is.

Preston collected the
money from his desk
and was coming out
of the school when

suddenly!

Preston decided to use the back door.

On his way back to the shop
Preston stopped at the park
to have a little play when

Billy the bully
shoved past him and
went down the slide!

Preston climbed down
from the slide and went
to do the shopping.
He was just coming out
of the shop when

suddenly!

Mr Plimp the shopkeeper
called Preston back to
say he had forgotten
his change.

At last Preston arrived home. "Mum," he said. "I've had the strangest feeling that someone has been following me."

Suddenly!

Preston's Mum turned around
and gave him an enormous

cuddle!

Collect all the Preston Pig Stories

Colin McNaughton
Suddenly!
Look behind you, Preston Pig!
0-00-714013-4

Colin McNaughton
GOAL!
Go football crazy with Preston Pig!
0-00-714011-8

Colin McNaughton
BOO!
Surprise! It's Preston Pig!
0-00-714014-2

Colin McNaughton
Oops!
I'm coming to get you, Preston Pig!
0-00-714015-0

Colin McNaughton
Shh!
(Don't Tell Mister Wolf)
A Preston Pig Lift-the-Flap Book
0-00-664715-4

Colin McNaughton
Hmm...
Who's hungry for Preston Pig?
0-00-714012-6

Colin McNaughton
OompH!
Fall in love with Preston Pig!
0-00-712635-2

Colin McNaughton
little Suddenly!
a Preston Pig toddler book
0-00-713235-2

Colin McNaughton
little Oops!
a Preston Pig toddler book
0-00-713236-0

Colin McNaughton
little Goal!
a Preston Pig toddler book
0-00-713234-4

Colin McNaughton
little Boo!
a Preston Pig toddler book
0-00-713237-9

Colin McNaughton
WHEE!
A Preston Pig TV Story
0-00-712371-X

Colin McNaughton
POOH!
A Preston Pig TV Story
0-00-712370-1

Colin McNaughton
PARP!
A Preston Pig TV Story
0-00-712372-8

Colin McNaughton is one of Britain's most highly-acclaimed picture book talents and a winner of many prestigious awards. His Preston Pig Stories are hugely successful with Preston now starring in his own animated television series on CITV.